Ms Wiz Spells Trouble

In Stitches With Ms Wiz

You're Nicked, Ms Wiz

Terence Blacker

Illustrated by Tony Ross

MACMILLAN CHILDREN'S BOOKS

Ms Wiz Spells Trouble
First published 1988 by Piccadilly Press Ltd
Young Piper edition published 1989 by Pan Books
This edition published 1996 by Macmillan Children's Books
In Stitches With Ms Wiz
First published 1989 by Piccadilly Press Ltd
Young Piper edition published 1990 by Pan Books
This edition published 1996 by Macmillan Children's Books
You're Nicked, Ms Wiz
First published 1989 by Piccadilly Press Ltd
Young Piper edition published 1990 by Pan Books
This edition published 1996 by Macmillan Children's Books

This omnibus edition published 2004 by Macmillan Children's Books
A division of Macmillan Publishers Limited
20 New Wharf Road, London N1 9RR
Basingstoke and Oxford
www.panmacmillan.com

Associated companies throughout the world

ISBN 0 330 43136 6

3 5 7 9 8 6 4 2

A CIP catalogue record for this book is available from
the British Library.

Typeset by Intype Libra Ltd
Printed and bound in Great Britain by Mackays of Chatham plc, Kent

Ms Wiz
Spells Trouble

CHAPTER ONE

A New Arrival

Most teachers are strange and the teachers at St Barnabas School were no exception.

Yet it's almost certain that none of them – not Mr Gilbert, the head teacher, who liked to pick his nose during Assembly, not Mrs Hicks who talked to her teddies in class, not Miss Gomaz who smoked cigarettes in the lavatory – *none* of them was quite as odd as Class Three's new teacher.

Some of the children in Class Three thought she was a witch. Others said she was a hippy. A few of them thought she was just a bit mad. But they all agreed that there had never been anyone quite like her at St Barnabas before.

This is her story. I wonder what *you* think she was . . .

As soon as their new teacher walked into the classroom on the first day of term, the children of Class Three sensed that there was something different about her. She was quite tall, with long black hair and bright green eyes. She wore tight jeans and a purple blouse. Her fingers were decorated with several large rings and black nail varnish. She looked as if she were on her way to a disco, not teaching at a school.

Most surprising of all, she wasn't frightened. Class Three was known in the school as the "problem class". It had a reputation for being difficult and noisy, for having what was called a "disruptive element". Miss Jones, their last teacher, had left the school in tears. But none of that seemed to

worry this strange-looking new teacher.

"My name is Miss Wisdom," she said in a quiet but firm voice. "So what do you say to me every morning when I walk in?"

"Good morning, Miss Wisdom," said Class Three unenthusiastically.

"Wrong," said the teacher with a flash of her green eyes, "You say 'Hi, Ms Wiz!' "

Jack, who was one of Class Three's Disruptive Element, giggled at the back of the class.

"Yo," he said in a silly American accent. "Why, hi Ms Wiz!"

Caroline, the class dreamer, was paying attention for a change.

"Why is it Ms . . . er, Ms?" she asked.

"Well," said Ms Wiz, "I'm not a Mrs because I'm not married, thank goodness, and I'm not Miss because I think Miss sounds silly for a grown woman, don't you?"

"Not as silly as Ms," muttered Katrina, who liked to find fault wherever possible.

"And why Wiz?" asked a rather large boy sitting in the front row. It was Podge, who was probably the most annoying and certainly the greediest boy in the class.

"Wiz?" said Ms Wiz with a mysterious smile. "Just you wait and see."

Ms Wiz reached inside a big leather bag that she had placed beside her desk. She pulled out a china cat.

"That," she said, placing the cat carefully on her desk, "is my friend Hecate the Cat. She's watching you all the time. She sees everything and hears everything. She's my spy."

Ms Wiz turned to the blackboard.

"Weird," muttered Jack.

An odd, hissing sound came from

7

the china cat. Its eyes lit up like
torches.

"Hecate sees you even when my
back is turned," said Ms Wiz, who
now faced the class. "Will the person
who said 'weird' spell it please?"

Everyone stared at Jack, who
blushed.

"I.T.," he stammered.

No one laughed.

"Er, W . . . I . . ."

"Wrong," said Ms Wiz. "W.E.I.R.D.

If you don't know how to spell a word, Jack, don't use it." She patted the china cat.

"Good girl, Hecate," she said.

"How did she know my name?" whispered Jack.

The new teacher smiled. "Children, remember one thing. Ms Wiz knows everything."

"Now," she said briskly. "Pay attention, please. Talking of spelling, I'm going to give you a first lesson in casting spells."

"Oh great," said Katrina grumpily. "Now we've got a witch for a teacher."

Hecate the Cat hissed angrily.

"No, Katrina, not a witch," said Ms Wiz sharply. "We don't call them witches these days. It gives people the wrong idea. We call them Paranormal Operatives. Now – any suggestions for our first spell?"

Podge put up his hand immediately.

"Could we turn our crayons into lollipops, please Ms?" he asked.

"No," said Ms Wiz. "Spells are not for personal greed."

"How about turning Class Two into frogs?" asked Katrina.

"Nor are they for revenge. There will be no unpleasant spells around here while I'm your teacher," said Ms Wiz before adding, almost as an

afterthought, "unless they're deserved, of course."

She looked out of the window. In the playground Mr Brown, the school caretaker, was sweeping up leaves.

"Please draw the playground," said Ms Wiz. "Imagine it without any leaves. The best picture will create the spell."

Almost for the first time in living memory, Class Three worked in complete quiet. Katrina didn't

complain that someone had nicked her pencil. Caroline managed to concentrate on her work. Podge forgot to look in his trouser pocket for one last sweet. Not a single paper pellet was shot across the room by Jack.

At the end of the lesson, Ms Wiz looked at the drawings carefully.

"Well, they're all quite good," she said eventually. "But I think I like Caroline's the best."

She took Caroline's drawing and carefully taped it to the window.

"Please close your eyes while I cast the spell," she said.

There was a curious humming noise as Class Three sat, eyes closed, in silence.

"Open," said Ms Wiz, after a few seconds. "Regard Caroline's work."

The children looked at Caroline's drawing. It was steaming slightly and, in one corner, there was a freshly drawn pile of leaves.

"Hey – look at the playground!" shouted Katrina.

Everyone looked out of the window. To their amazement, the leaves on the ground had disappeared. Mr Brown stood by his wheelbarrow, scratching his head.

"Weird," said Jack. "Very weird indeed."

CHAPTER TWO

"Ms Wiz is Magic"

"Yes, I'm afraid she is a bit odd," sighed the head teacher, Mr Gilbert, as he took tea one morning with Miss Gomaz and Mrs Hicks in the Staff Common Room.

"Those jeans," sniffed Miss Gomaz. "And I never thought I'd live to see *black* nail-varnish at St Barnabas."

"But you have to admit she seems to have Class Three under control," said Mr Gilbert. "That's a whole week she's been here and not one child has been sent to my study. Not one window has been broken."

Mrs Hicks stirred her tea disapprovingly.

"It won't last," she said. "The Disruptive Element will get the better of her. And there are some very

14

strange noises coming from that classroom."

"I'd keep an eye on the situation if I were you, head teacher," said Miss Gomaz.

Mr Gilbert sighed.

"Yes," he said wearily. "That's what I'll do. Keep an eye on the situation."

The fact is that Class Three, including the Disruptive Element, were having the time of their lives.

Every lesson with Ms Wiz was different.

"Now, Class Three," she would say, "I'm going to teach you something rather unusual. But remember – what happens in this classroom is our secret. The magic only works if nobody except us knows about it."

Surprisingly, Class Three agreed.

So no one – not even parents or

other children at the school – had any idea of the strange things that happened to Class Three.

They never heard how Caroline's picture of the playground saved Mr Brown a morning's work.

They never heard how Jack's desk moved to the front of the class all by itself when Hecate spotted him talking at the back.

They never heard how Katrina flew around the class three times on a

vacuum cleaner after she had complained that Ms Wiz couldn't be a real witch – sorry, Paranormal Operative – because she didn't ride a broomstick.

They never heard about the nature lesson when the class met Herbert, a pet rat that Ms Wiz kept up her sleeve.

But they did hear about the day when Podge became the hero of the class.

Nobody could keep *that* a secret.

Once every term, Class Three played a football match against a team from a school nearby, called Brackenhurst. It was a very important game and everyone from St Barnabas gathered in the playground to watch. Last term, Class Three had lost 10–0.

"That was because Miss Jones

picked all the wimps," explained Jack.

"Because she was a wimp herself," said Caroline.

The rest of the class agreed noisily.

"I'll be manager," shouted Jack over the din.

Ms Wiz held up her hands like a wizard about to cast a spell.

"I'll be manager," she said firmly.

"But you don't know anything about football," said Jack.

"Ms Wiz knows everything," said Caroline.

"Creep!" muttered Katrina.

Hecate the Cat hissed angrily.

"All right, Hecate," said Katrina quickly. "I take it back."

"My team," said Ms Wiz, "is Jack, Simon, Katrina, Alex and . . ."

She looked around the classroom and saw Podge's arm waving wildly.

"No, Ms Wiz," several of the class

shouted at once. "Not Podge! He's useless!"

"... and Podge."

There was a groan from around the classroom.

"Here comes another hammering," said Jack gloomily.

For a while during the game that afternoon, it looked as though Jack's prediction had been right. After three minutes, Brackenhurst had already scored twice. Podge had been a disaster, falling over his own feet every time the ball came near him.

"Serves that Ms Cleverclogs right," said Mrs Hicks, who was watching the match with Miss Gomaz. "Look at her, jumping up and down like that, making herself look foolish in front of the kiddies. Anybody would think she was a child herself."

"It's embarrassing, that's what it

is," agreed Miss Gomaz.

"*Do* something," said Caroline who was standing next to Ms Wiz.

"And what do you suggest, Caroline?" asked Ms Wiz whose normally pale face was now quite red.

"You know," whispered Caroline. "Something *special*."

"Oh, all right," sighed Ms Wiz. "I suppose a *little* magic wouldn't hurt."

At that moment, Podge blundered

into one of the Brackenhurst's players and knocked him over. Mr Gilbert, who was referee, blew hard on his whistle for a free kick against Class Three – but not a sound came out. In fact, the only sound to be heard was a faint humming noise from the direction of Ms Wiz.

"That's better," said Caroline.

Brackenhurst's players were still waiting for the whistle to blow when Podge set off with the ball at his feet. He took two paces and booted it wildly. It was heading several feet wide of the Brackenhurst goal when, to everyone's astonishment, the ball changed direction and, as if it had a life of its own, flew into the back of the net.

For a moment, there was a stunned silence. Then Ms Wiz could be heard cheering on her team once more.

"What a shot!" she shouted. "Nice one, Podge!"

"Appalling behaviour," muttered Mrs Hicks.

From then on, the game altered completely. Not even in his wildest dreams, when he had scored the winning goal for Spurs in the FA Cup Final, had Podge played so well.

Soon even Jack was shouting, "Give it to Podge! Give the ball to Podge!" while the Brackenhurst players were screaming, "Stop the fat one! Trip him, someone!"

But nobody could stop Podge. Playing as if he were under a spell, he scored three goals to give Class Three a great 3–2 victory.

After the game, the class gathered around Ms Wiz, shouting, cheering and singing songs.

"So much for her having her class under control," said Mrs Hicks. "They may win matches but Class Three are worse than ever with the new teacher."

24

Miss Gomaz had hurried over to Mr Gilbert.

"Just look at that, head teacher," she said, pointing to Class Three, who were now singing "Ms Wiz is magic!" at the top of their voices. "It's nothing short of anarchy."

But Mr Gilbert wasn't listening. He was still studying his new whistle and wondering why it hadn't worked.

CHAPTER THREE

An Extremely
Mathematical Owl

"This is all very difficult," said Mr Gilbert, puffing nervously on his pipe. He was sitting in his study with Ms Wiz, who at this moment was looking at him with an annoying little smile on her face. "Very awkward. You see, Miss Wisdom – er, Ms Wiz – there have been, well, complaints."

"Goodness," said Ms Wiz brightly. "What on earth about?"

Mr Gilbert fumbled around with his pipe. Why *was* he feeling so nervous? Of course, he was always uneasy with women, but there were lots of women who were more frightening than Ms Wiz – Mrs Gilbert, for a start. The thought of his wife made the head teacher sit up in his armchair and try again.

"Firstly, there have been complaints about the way you look," he said, glancing at Ms Wiz. She was actually wearing black lipstick today.

"You find something wrong with the way I look?" asked Ms Wiz, who was beginning to be confused by this conversation.

"No, no," said Mr Gilbert, tapping his pipe on an ashtray. "I like . . . I mean, I don't . . . personally . . . Then," he said, quickly changing the subject, "there's what you teach. Your history lessons, for example."

"But Class Three loves history," said Ms Wiz. "We're doing the French Revolution at the moment."

"So I gather," said Mr Gilbert. "The entire class was walking around the playground yesterday shouting, 'Behead the aristocrats!' I'm told that Jack was carrying a potato on the end of a sharp stick."

Ms Wiz laughed. "They're very keen," she said.

"Perhaps you could move on to some other part of history – *nice* history," said the head teacher. "1066, the Armada, King Alfred and the cakes."

"Oh no," said Ms Wiz. "We already have our next project."

"May I know what it is?" asked Mr Gilbert uneasily.

"Certainly," said Ms Wiz. "The Great Fire of London."

The head teacher gulped. Mrs Hicks and Miss Gomaz had been right. Ms Wiz spelt trouble.

"Perhaps," he said, "you could concentrate on some other subject for the time being."

"Of course," said Ms Wiz. "We'll try a spot of maths for a while."

Mr Gilbert smiled for the first time that morning.

"Perfect," he said.

Maths, he thought to himself after Ms Wiz had left his study. That couldn't cause trouble. Could it?

"Now, Class Three," said Ms Wiz that afternoon. "I'm going to test you on your nine times table – multiplication and division."

There was a groan around the classroom. Nobody liked the nine times table.

"And to help me," continued Ms Wiz, "I've brought my friend Archimedes." She reached inside her desk and brought out a large white owl. "Archie's what they call a bit of a number-cruncher. He loves his tables," she said, putting the owl on top of the blackboard.

"Cats, rats and now owls," muttered Katrina. "This place gets more like a zoo every day."

"Archie is a barn owl," said Ms

Wiz, ignoring Katrina. "An extremely mathematical barn owl. Place the waste-paper basket beneath him please, Caroline."

"Why, Ms Wiz?" asked Caroline.

"Wait and see," said Ms Wiz.

Caroline put the waste-paper basket beneath Archie who was now looking around the classroom, blinking wisely.

"Now Podge," said Ms Wiz. "Tell Archie what five nines are."

"Forty-five," said Podge.

"Toowoo," went Archie.

"That means correct," said Ms Wiz. "Simon – nine nines."

"Eighty one," said Simon.

"Toowoo."

"Now Jack," said Ms Wiz. "Let's try division. A boy has 108 marbles. He divides them between his nine friends. What does that make?"

"It makes him a wally for giving away all his marbles," said Jack.

31

Archie looked confused.

"Try again, Jack," said Ms Wiz patiently.

"Erm . . . eleven."

Class Three looked at Archie expectantly. Without a sound, the owl lifted its tail and did something very nasty into the waste-paper basket beneath him.

"Uuuuuuurrrrggghhhh, gross," said the children. "He's done a—"

"The correct word is guano," said Ms Wiz. "Jack?"

"Ten," said Jack.

Archie lifted his tail.

"Eight."

Archie did it again.

"How does he keep doing that?" asked Podge.

Ms Wiz shrugged. "He's well trained," she said.

"We'd better have another basket standing by," said Katrina. "Jack's never going to get it."

"He'd better," said Ms Wiz firmly. "Every time Archie is obliged to do his ... guano, it means fifty lines."

Jack groaned. "Um ..."

Outside the door Mrs Hick and Miss Gomaz were listening carefully.

They had left their classes with some reading work and were determined to catch the new teacher doing something wrong.

"Listen to that noise," said Miss Gomaz. "It's an absolute disgrace."

"Let's take a look through the window from the playground," said Miss Hicks.

Moments later, the two teachers were watching in amazement as Jack struggled to give Archie the correct answer.

"There's a bird on the blackboard," whispered Miss Gomaz.

"It's . . . it's going to the lavatory,"

gasped Mrs Hicks. "In a bin. I can't believe my eyes."

They were just pressing their noses to the window-pane to get a closer look when Ms Wiz glanced up. Those at the front of the class could hear a slight hum coming from her direction.

"Miss Gomaz! Miss Gomaz!" said Mrs Hicks. "My nose! It's stuck to the glass!"

"Mine too!" cried Miss Gomaz,

trying to pull back from the window-pane. "Ouch! That hurts!"

It was at that moment that the bell rang for afternoon break. Soon the teachers were surrounded by laughing children.

"Don't just stand there, you horrible children," screamed Mrs Hicks. "Get help quickly!"

"No need," said Ms Wiz, who had joined the children in the playground. She tapped the glass. Miss Gomaz and Mrs Hicks fell back, free at last.

"It must have been the frost," said Ms Wiz, with an odd little smile.

"Frost?" said Miss Gomaz, rubbing her nose. "At this time of year? Don't talk daft."

"It's only September," said Mrs Hicks.

"Yes," said Ms Wiz. "What funny old weather we've been having, don't you think?"

CHAPTER FOUR

Herbert Takes a Wrong Turning

It was during an art lesson that Class Three were first given an idea where Ms Wiz came from.

She had asked the children to draw an imaginary building. The project was called "The House of My Dreams".

Jack drew a house that looked like Wembley Stadium. It had a football pitch in the living room and all the walls were slanted like skateboard ramps.

Caroline drew the mansion that she would have when she became a film star. It had a huge lawn and swimming pool. In every room, there was a cocktail cabinet for drinks.

Podge drew Buckingham Palace

made out of milk chocolate and fudge.

Katrina drew a strange, dark cottage in a wood. Cats with shining eyes stood guard on each side of the front door and bats flew in and out of its old thatched roof. She called it "Ms Wiz's Magic Cottage".

When Katrina finished the picture, Ms Wiz laughed. "It's lovely," she said, "but not at all like where I really live."

"Where *do* you live?" asked Katrina. The entire class grew quiet. Somehow no one had ever dared ask Ms Wiz about herself before.

"I live in a flat a long, long way away," said Ms Wiz. "At a place where almost certainly none of you have been. It's on the outskirts of town."

"Can we come and visit you during the holidays?" asked Jack.

"During the holidays I'm doing

other things," said Ms Wiz. "That's my job – to go wherever a little magic is needed. Wherever," she smiled, "things need shaking up a little."

"You've certainly shaken things up at St Barnabas," said Katrina. "Does that mean you'll be leaving us soon?"

Ms Wiz smiled. "Katrina, I'll only leave you when you no longer need me."

For a moment, there was silence in Class Three. Then Podge put up his hand.

"If you live so far away," he asked, "how do you get to school every day? Do you fly on your vacuum cleaner?"

"No," said Ms Wiz. "I come by bus."

If Ms Wiz was a little more serious than usual that afternoon, it was because she was thinking of the evening ahead of her. It was Parents' Evening.

Ms Wiz liked being with children. She didn't even mind being with teachers. But the idea of a whole evening spent in the company of parents made her feel tired already.

"I must remember to keep my spells under control," she said to herself as she waited for the first parent to arrive. "Adults aren't like children. Magic seems to upset them."

The door opened.

"I'm Harris," said a large man in a suit, who was the first parent to arrive. He shook Ms Wiz firmly by the hand. "Peter's dad. This," he nodded curtly towards a nervous-looking woman standing a pace behind him, "is Mother."

Peter? Ms Wiz's mind raced. Who was Peter? Of course – that was Podge's real name.

"Pod – I mean Peter is doing well

40

this term," she said, glancing at her notes.

"We're not happy," said Mr Harris firmly. "Isn't that right, Mother?"

"It is," said Mrs Harris. "We're not happy at all."

"The lad's gone strange on us," continued Mr Harris. "Always got his head in a book. Or talking about school. Asking us questions about this and that when his mother and I are trying to watch telly."

"Questions all the time," said Mrs Harris.

"Yak yak yak," said Mr Harris. "I'm a busy man. I work at the Town Hall. I want to relax of an evening, not answer questions from my own flesh and blood. That's your job."

Ms Wiz smiled. "Perhaps it's a good sign that he's interested in—"

"He's never been interested before. Tea, telly, bed was our way. Nothing wrong with that." Mr Harris leant forward angrily. "I've said to Mother and I'll say it to you. I smell a rat –" (for a horrible moment, Ms Wiz thought he had discovered Herbert, who was asleep up her sleeve) – "and when Cuthbert Harris smells a rat, heads will roll. Come on, Mother, I'm off."

Mr Harris stood up and, without another word, walked towards the door. Was it an accident that a banana skin had been left on the floor – or was it a touch of Ms Wiz magic after all?

"Woooaaaahhh!"

With a sickening crash, Mr Harris landed on the floor in a heap.

"Oh, Cuthbert!" said Mrs Harris. "Your best suit!"

Podge's father stood up, red-faced.

"Right! That's it!" he said as he dusted himself down. "Town Hall's going to hear of this. Heads will roll!"

Ms Wiz sighed as the door slammed behind Mr and Mrs Harris. Yes, she definitely preferred children to parents.

Ms Wiz was not often angry but when, a few days after Parents' Evening, Mr Gilbert brought a School Inspector from the Town Hall into the classroom, there was an unusual sharpness in her tone when she addressed the class.

"Now sit up, Class Three," she said after the head teacher had left the School Inspector sitting at a little desk at the back of the class. "Remember we're being inspected today."

The School Inspector pursed his lips and made a note on the pad in front of him.

It was a quiet lesson without, of course, a hint of magic. Even Hecate the Cat remained hidden in Ms Wiz's bag.

Unfortunately nobody had told Herbert that Class Three was being inspected and Herbert, as luck would have it, decided on this particular moment to explore the classroom.

After a few minutes of the lesson, he had discovered a new tunnel. It was warm and dark, like a very inviting, old-fashioned chimney.

Who could blame him for wanting to explore it? Rats like chimneys.

45

How was he to know that he was climbing up the left leg of the School Inspector's trousers?

At first the School Inspector twitched. Then he shifted nervously in his seat. Then, as Herbert edged his way past his knee and upwards, the School Inspector stood up.

"Oh . . . ooh . . . ," he said, patting his thigh. "What the . . . oh . . . ah . . ." He hopped around the classroom. It was then that Herbert decided

the chimney was moving around rather too much for comfort – and made for the safety of the School Inspector's underpants.

"AAAARRRRRGGGGGHHHHH!"

The School Inspector tore at his belt, jumped out of his trousers and ran from the classroom.

Class Three watched in amazement as the half-naked figure sprinted across the playground, out of the school gates and down the road.

Relieved that the earthquake had passed, Herbert emerged nervously from the School Inspector's trousers on the classroom floor.

"Oh, Herbert," said Ms Wiz. "You've done it now."

CHAPTER FIVE

An Absolute Disgrace

Mr Gilbert was in a muddle. You might thing that Mr Gilbert was always in a muddle, but this was the biggest muddle he had ever been in since he became head teacher of St Barnabas.

He was in such a muddle that his bald head had developed ugly red blotches. His attention would wander during lessons. He had even stopped picking his nose during Assembly.

"I'm on the horns of a dilemma," he told Mrs Gilbert one evening. "People keep telling me that Ms Wiz is a disaster. Miss Gomaz and Mrs Hicks say she's a troublemaker. The School Inspector says her classroom is a health hazard. Mr Harris says heads will roll. They all want me to suspend her before the end-of-term prizegiving next week."

"Suspend her then, Henry," said Mrs Gilbert. "What's the problem?"

"The problem is that the children of Class Three have won all the prizes this term. It's incredible. That sleepy Caroline has won the Art Prize. The A for Attitude Award for Good Behaviour has gone to Katrina of all people. Even the appalling Podge has won a Commendation for his story, 'The Enchanted Fudge Cake with a Thick Creamy Milk Chocolate Filling'. How on earth can I say, 'Well done everyone in Class Three and by the way I'm suspending your teacher'?"

"You'd better do what you think is best," said Mrs Gilbert. "But don't allow yourself to be bullied this time."

"Of course not," said Mr Gilbert. "You know where I stand on bullying."

"Let me guess," said Mrs Gilbert.
"On the horns of a dilemma?"

"Precisely," said Mr Gilbert.

"It is true that you're going to be
suspended?" asked Katrina the next
day in class. "Ever since the School
Inspector lost his trousers, Mr
Gilbert's been giving you some very
funny looks."

"So have Miss Gomaz and Mrs
Hicks," said Jack. "They look
positively happy."

"My dad's smiling a lot," said
Podge. "And that's never a good
sign."

"Never you mind about me," said
Ms Wiz. "I can look after myself."

"Yeah," said Simon. "You can magic
'em. That would show 'em."

"What have I always said? No
unpleasant spells," said Ms Wiz.

"Oh, Ms,' said Podge. "Couldn't

you just use a bit of magic – just one little spell on Mr Gilbert?"

"Maybe you could change him into a human being," suggested Jack.

There were cheers around the classroom. Ms Wiz held up her hands. Class Three were quiet.

"No," she said. "I refuse to listen to rumours. If the head teacher no longer requires my services, there's nothing to be done about it."

"Oh yes, there is," said Jack.

Which is how Class Three's Great Plan came into being.

End-of-term prizegiving was the most important event of the term for St Barnabas. It took place on the last day before the holidays and everybody was there.

On the platform in the School Hall sat Mr Gilbert, the School Inspector, all the teachers and the Lady

Mayoress, a large, impressive woman who was wearing a large, impressive hat. In the audience were the children with their parents.

Mr Gilbert had just finished his end-of-term speech which, give or take a couple of pathetic jokes, was the same as every end-of-term speech he had made for the last ten years.

"Now," he said, "I would like to ask the Lady Mayoress—" Mr Gilbert gave a simpering little bow in her direction "—to present the prizes. First, the Art Prize to Caroline Smith of Class Three."

There was polite applause as Caroline collected her prize.

"The Maths Prize has been won by Jack Beddows of Class Three."

Jack collected his prize, giving a modest wave to his supporters from the platform.

"The A for Attitude Award for Good Behaviour—" Mr Gilbert tried

to keep the disbelief out of his voice, "to Katrina O'Brien of Class Three." Katrina actually gave a little curtsey to the Lady Mayoress as she was presented with her award.

"And Specially Commended for his essay, 'The Enchanted Fudge Cake with a Thick Creamy Milk Chocolate Filling' – Peter Harris of Class Three."

Podge climbed the steps to the platform. But instead of collecting his prize from the Lady Mayoress, he took the microphone from the astonished head teacher.

"Everyone in Class Three wants to thank Ms Wiz," he announced. "She's the best teacher we've ever had—"

"Give me that microphone, boy," said Mr Gilbert, chasing Podge around the stage.

"WE HOPE SHE NEVER EVER LEAVES!" shouted Podge. "Don't we, Class Three?"

At that moment, the children of Class Three stood up and started cheering. Several of them produced banners, reading "MS WIZ IS MAGIC" and "NO SACK FOR MS WIZ", which had been smuggled into the hall.

"You can stop that right now, Peter," said Podge's father, Mr Harris, advancing towards the platform. "I'm going to give you a proper larrupping when you get home."

There was a humming sound from the back of the stage where Ms Wiz was sitting quietly.

Suddenly Mr Harris had turned into a strange pig-like animal.

"Goodness," said Miss Gomaz. "He's turned into a warthog."

"Surely not," said Mrs Hicks. "Warthogs don't have those funny little tusks. He looks more like a wild boar to me."

"Never mind that," shouted Mr

Gilbert. "We have a full-scale riot on our baaa—" In a flash, there was a sheep standing in the head teacher's place.

By now the entire school was chanting, "We want Ms Wiz! We want Ms Wiz!"

Ms Wiz stood up and Podge gave her the microphone.

"I think," she said firmly, "that we should continue prizegiving in half an hour. I'd like to see Class Three in their classroom now, please."

She made her way through the audience, which was now silent.

"Phone the police, Miss Gomaz," hissed Mrs Hicks.

Ms Wiz glanced over her shoulder.

Suddenly where Miss Gomaz and Mrs Hicks had been standing, there were two grey geese, making a furious gobbling noise.

*

"That was very kind of you, Class Three," said Ms Wiz, when all the children had gathered in the classroom. "But the fact is, I'm leaving St Barnabas anyway."

There was silence in the classroom.

"Why?" asked Katrina eventually.

"After all that," muttered Podge.

"I go where magic is needed," said Ms Wiz. "Where things need livening up. Today you've proved that you no

longer need me. You're the best class in the school."

'We won't be, without you," said Caroline.

"Yes, you will," said Ms Wiz. "Wait and see."

"We'll miss you," said Jack, serious for once.

"No, you won't because . . ."

The class looked expectantly at Ms Wiz. Caroline managed to stop sniffling at the back of the class.

". . . because I'll be back," said Ms Wiz.

"When?"

"Where?"

"Next term?"

Ms Wiz held up her hands.

"I'll come back and see each one of you," she said with a smile. "When you least expect it, when you need a spot of Ms Wiz in your life, I'll be there."

"Every one of us?" asked Simon.

"Every one of you," said Ms Wiz. "And I'll bring Hecate the Cat and Herbert."

Ms Wiz gathered up her bag. She swung her leg over her vacuum cleaner, like a cowboy about to ride out of town on his horse.

"Go back to the School Hall and finish prizegiving," she said. "You'll find everything's back to normal."

Ms Wiz hovered in mid-air by the classroom window.

"See you soon, Class Three," she said and flew off across the playground and over the School Hall.

"Oh no," said Jack as the class filed back into the hall. "Look who Ms Wiz has forgotten."

On the platform beside Mr Gilbert, the School Inspector and the Lady Mayoress, who were looking as if nothing strange had happened at all, stood two grey geese.

"She'll *have* to come back now," said Katrina.

"No unpleasant spells," said Podge.

They heard a familiar hum from outside the hall.

"Gobble gobble gobble – absolute disgrace," said Miss Gomaz.

Jack sighed.

"I think I preferred them as geese," he said.

IN STITCHES WITH
MS WIZ

CHAPTER ONE
A Pain on Thursday

Have you ever seen an ambulance racing at top speed through the streets, overtaking cars, driving through red traffic lights, its siren blaring and its blue light flashing? Have you ever thought that it would be exciting to be riding in the back, behind the darkened windows of the ambulance?

Well, it isn't.

Jack Beddows loved going fast – he had always thought that he would like to be a fireman or policeman one day so that he could break the speed limit whenever he felt like it – but right now, as he lay in the back of an ambulance travelling at sixty miles an hour down a busy street, he

wasn't interested. In fact, he would have given anything to be back at home, lying in his bed, without this terrible pain in his stomach.

It was the worst stomach ache of all time and it had been getting more painful all day. It was so bad that he hadn't been able to concentrate at school. In the middle of the maths lesson, he had even started crying.

"Please, sir." Jack's friend Caroline had put up her hand. "Jack's feeling ill."

The new teacher, Mr Bailey, had continued writing on the blackboard. "I'm not surprised," he had said. "I felt ill when I looked at his work this morning."

"But sir—" Caroline had protested.

"Nice try, Jack," said Mr Bailey. "Just in time for the maths test on Monday. Very convenient, I must say."

The ambulance took a corner with a screech of tyres. Jack groaned.

If only Ms Wiz had still been at school, he thought. She had been the class teacher last term and, whenever there were problems, she somehow made it better with her magic spells. There was certainly nothing magic about Mr Bailey.

When Jack hobbled home after school, he had found his father messing around with the car, as usual.

"Dad," Jack had said to the pair of legs sticking out from under the car. "I've got a pain in my stomach."

His father continued working. "Have you been?" he asked eventually.

That was the sum total of his father's medical knowledge. Even when his little sister Jenny had complained of having toothache, it had been the same old question. Have you been?

By the time his mother had come back from the library where she worked, Jack had been sick twice.

"Down in the dumps?" she had asked cheerfully. "A bit under the weather?"

"No. Ill."

"Why not go and skateboard outside?"

"I'm too ill to skateboard."

"Ring the doctor, Dad," said Mrs Beddows. "I think it's serious."

It certainly felt serious, Jack thought as the ambulance finally came to a halt. The doors swung open. Jack was put on a trolley and wheeled into the hospital.

The nurse in the main hall looked

down at Jack. "How are we?" she asked.

Jack smiled weakly. "We're not very well," he said.

"Children's ward," said the nurse to the man pushing Jack's trolley. "The doctor will be right along. I'll get them to prepare the theatre."

Theatre? thought Jack as he was wheeled into a brightly-coloured ward. Here I am, dying, and they're

talking about t[...]

The other chil[...] stared as a nurse [...] around Jack's bed.

"Just slip out of y[...] said, "and pop into t[...]

She gave Jack what [...] nightie.

"I'm a boy," he protes[...]d feebly.

"And this is a gown," said the nurse. "Hurry up. The Consultant

will be here in [...]
Jack had [...]
a tall [...]
his [...]

a minute."

. . . just put on his gown when
. . . an with a white coat poked
. . . head around the curtains. The
Consultant stood by Jack's bed and
looked down at him like a vulture
considering its breakfast. Behind him
stood another doctor. She had her
dark hair in a bun and wore rather
peculiar glasses. Something about the
way she smiled at him reminded Jack
of someone he knew.

"Let's have a quick look at you,"
said the Consultant, pressing the
right side of Jack's stomach with his
cold hands.

"Ow," said Jack.

"Mm. Uncomfortable?"

"Yes," said Jack.

The Consultant turned to the nurse.

"Are the parents here?" he asked.

"They've been delayed," she said.
"Apparently they were trying to

follow the ambulance and had a small disagreement with a double-decker bus. They're all right. They rang to give their permission to operate."

Jack groaned. His first time in hospital and his father had driven into a bus while chasing the ambulance. Typical.

"We're going to give you a little operation," the Consultant said to Jack, as if it were some kind of treat. "We need to take out your appendix to make you feel better."

"What's an appendix?"

"It's a small, completely useless piece of gristle in your intestine," said the Consultant. "I promise you won't miss it. Now we'd better hurry because that naughty appendix really ought to come out soon."

That's just great, thought Jack, as he was wheeled off once again. I'm about to be cut open by someone who talks about a naughty appendix.

There was something else bothering him. It was the other doctor. Now where had he seen her before? He wished she were doing the operation. A lot of people smiled at the hospital but she was different – she looked as if she meant it.

"Mr Jones here is what we call the anaesthetist," said the Consultant when Jack arrived in another room. "He's going to give you a little prick in the arm and you'll fall asleep."

Was Jack dreaming already? The woman doctor had seemed to give him an enormous wink, as if they were old friends. As the anaesthetist bent over his arm, there was a familiar humming noise. The needle of the injection suddenly bent over, like a wilting flower.

It couldn't be, could it? Jack looked at her more closely. The hair was

different and she never used to have
glasses, but there was something
about the black nail varnish she was
wearing. Now where had he seen
black nail varnish?

"Funny," said the anaesthetist,
reaching for another needle.

"A lot of funny things are
happening in this hospital at the
moment," said the Consultant.
"Aren't they, Doctor Wisdom?"

Doctor Wisdom! It must be! She

had promised she'd see him again.
What were her exact words? "I go
wherever magic is needed." He
certainly needed magic now.

Jack felt the injection go into his
arm. He heard a voice saying, "Now
just count to three."

"Hi, Ms . . . Wiiiii . . ."

And Jack was fast asleep.

CHAPTER TWO

Magic on Friday

Hospitalized!

The word spread like wildfire through St Barnabas School the day after Jack was taken into hospital. The Morris twins, who knew the family that lived next door to him, said he would be away from school for days. By break time, the rumour was that he would miss the rest of term. By lunch, it was generally agreed that Jack was unlikely ever to be seen at school again.

"What's 'hospitalized', sir?" Caroline asked Mr Bailey during Class Three's first lesson.

"It means that someone has to go into hospital," said the teacher, with a sympathetic smile. "Why, Caroline? Is it someone in your family?"

"It's Jack, sir. You remember that pain he had, sir – in maths?"

"Jack?" Mr Bailey looked worried. "I can't remember any pain."

"Siiir!" There were protests of disbelief from around the classroom.

"Yes, yes, all right. I remember now."

"Well, it got worse and worse," said

Caroline, who was beginning to enjoy herself now. "By the end of the day, he was *screaming* in agony."

"Don't be ridiculous, Caroline," said Mr Bailey nervously. "Er . . . really?"

"Hospitalized," said Caroline dramatically. She stared at Jack's empty seat. "Apparently the doctors only had one question. '*Why wasn't this child brought to us sooner?*' There's

going to be an investigation."

Mr Bailey had turned very pale.

"Um. Just got to visit the head teacher," he said, scurrying to the door with an anxious, hunted look. "Revise for your maths test, everyone. I'll be back in a minute."

The first time Jack woke up after his operation, he felt dizzy and sick. There was a tube sticking into his arm, he had a pain in his side, and his parents were talking at him.

Thinking that he almost preferred the stomach ache, he drifted off to sleep.

The second time Jack woke up after his operation, it was evening and his parents had gone home, but Ms Wiz was standing beside his bed.

"Ms Wiz!" Jack said weakly.

"Dr Wisdom at your service. I

thought you might be needing some special magic."

"Can you make me feel better?"

"I can't do that," said Ms Wiz, drawing the curtains around Jack's bed, "but I might be able to cheer you up a bit."

She reached into an inside pocket of her white coat and pulled out a china cat.

"Here's Hecate to look after you," she said, putting the cat on the bedside table. "Any time you need me, just tap her on the head."

"Thanks," croaked Jack.

"And you'll be needing some company," said Ms Wiz, putting her hand into another pocket and pulling out her tame, magic rat. "So Herbert will be staying with you until you're better."

She put Herbert the rat on to the bed. He sniffed around a bit and was about to scurry under the bedclothes when Ms Wiz said, "Not there, Herbert – it's unhygienic. Under the pillow."

"But—" Jack tried to concentrate. "How did you get here?"

"They were expecting a supply doctor, whom I happened to know was ill. So I just turned up. They're so desperate for doctors here that they never even asked to see my papers."

"Cool," said Jack.

"Now, remember," said Ms Wiz, tucking up the bed. "Don't tell any of the nurses or doctors about our secret. They may not like the idea of magic spells in a modern hospital. They might even think I'm a sort of witch."

"Can I tell the other children?"

Ms Wiz looked around the ward and smiled.

"Of course you can," she said.

*

"She's never a witch."

The boy in the bed next to Jack's was called Franklyn. He had a bad back and he didn't believe in magic.

"Witches are for wimps," he said.

There was a hiss from Hecate, the china cat, and her eyes lit up.

"Nice toy," said Franklyn, unimpressed. He picked up his football magazine and started leafing through it.

Jack was too tired to argue.

"Just you wait and see," he said.

The next morning, the children's ward was visited by the Consultant. There was a group of medical students with him.

"I took this young man's appendix out yesterday," said the Consultant, when he reached Jack's bed. He turned to Ms Wiz, who was standing

at the back of the group. "How is he, Dr Wisdom?"

"He's recovering well," said Ms Wiz, with a little smile in Jack's direction.

The Consultant turned to the students and took a small bottle from his pocket.

"And here," he said, "is the appendix in question. As you can see it was badly inflamed."

The students looked at the bottle

which seemed to contain a small red caterpillar, floating in liquid. The Consultant put the bottle down on the table beside Jack's bed.

"Let's have a look at the patient," he said. "Miss Harris, would you like to check his heart?"

One of the students stepped forward, put a stethoscope to her ears and placed the other end on Jack's heart. There was a faint humming noise from the direction of Ms Wiz. The student looked puzzled.

"Well?" said the Consultant. "What do you hear?"

"It seems to be disco music," said the student.

Jack winked at Franklyn who was now unable to hide his curiosity.

"Give me that stethoscope," said the Consultant. He listened to Jack's heart. "Extraordinary," he said.

"Excuse me," said Franklyn from the next bed. "There's a . . ."

But the Consultant was too busy looking at the stethoscope in his hand to pay any attention.

Jack now saw what Franklyn was staring at. Herbert the rat had escaped from under his pillow and, using the bedspread as cover, had made his way down to the foot of the bed. As the Consultant and his students examined the stethoscope, he peeped out, ran to where the little bottle containing Jack's appendix stood, picked it up in his mouth and scurried back under the bedclothes.

"Excuse me—" said Franklyn again.

Jack put a finger to his lips and shook his head slowly.

"Yes, Franklyn?" asked Ms Wiz innocently. "Is something the matter?"

"Er, maybe not," said Franklyn.

CHAPTER THREE

A Visit on Saturday

It was Saturday morning, Jack's third day without an appendix, and Caroline and Podge had been allowed by their parents to walk to the hospital to visit him.

"How you feeling, Jacko?" asked Podge.

"Not bad," said Jack. "Considering I've had a major operation."

"Major operation," sniffed Franklyn from the next bed. "All they did was take out a small, completely useless piece of gristle."

"Oh no!" Caroline looked shocked. "You mean it was a brain operation?"

Jack started to laugh, then clutched his stomach. "Don't," he said. "It hurts when I laugh."

"I've got to admit that he's an interesting neighbour," Franklyn went on. "He thinks his doctor is a witch."

Podge looked amazed. "It's not . . .?"

"It is," smiled Jack.

"*And* he's got a rat under his pillow," Franklyn continued loudly.

"Sshh!" said Jack. "Don't let anyone know or there'll be trouble."

"Ah," said Franklyn. "Problem. I

think I just did – about five minutes ago."

At that moment, there was a scream from the other end of the ward.

News travels fast in a hospital. Franklyn had told his other neighbour Katie, who was suffering from asthma. Katie had told Matthew, who was hanging upside down with two broken legs. Matthew

had told Michelle, who was having tests. Michelle had told Amber, who had just had her tonsils out. Amber had whispered it to Tom, who had grommets. Tom had told his mother – and that was the scream from the other end of the ward.

"Now children," said the Ward Sister, as Tom's mother recovered on a spare bed. "You may have heard that a small, furry animal has been seen in here . . ."

"She means a rat," said Franklyn. There was a moan from Tom's mother.

". . . and small, furry animals are not welcome in hospitals, even if they are pets. So the nurses are going to search the ward."

"What will you do if you find it?" asked Jack.

"Confiscate it, of course," said the Ward Sister. "We're lucky enough to have an experimental laboratory downstairs. They always need fresh mice and rats."

Caroline and Podge gasped. Jack calmly leant over and tapped Hecate the cat's head. Her eyes flashed.

"Morning, Sister," said Ms Wiz, who breezed into the ward within seconds.

"Morning, Dr Wisdom."

Ms Wiz glanced at the nurses as they looked under the beds and in cupboards.

"Goodness," she said. "What's going on here?"

The Ward Sister whispered something in her ear.

"A *rat*?" Ms Wiz seemed shocked. "In that case, I'll just check the Beddows boy's dressing and leave you to it."

Ms Wiz hurried over to Jack's bed and pulled the curtains around it.

"Up to your old tricks, eh Ms Wiz?" said Caroline quietly.

"Just trying to cheer Jack up," said Ms Wiz, feeling under his pillow, eventually pulling out Herbert.

"Have you got one of those cardboard bottle things?" she asked Jack.

"You don't mean—?"

"That's right. The little bottles they give you to pee in when you're in bed."

Jack passed it to Ms Wiz, who had just slipped Herbert into the bottle when the curtains drew back. It was the Ward Sister.

"Jack's been a good boy, has he?" she said, looking at the bottle in Ms Wiz's hands.

"Er, yes."

"Allow me, Doctor," said the Ward Sister, taking the bottle. "I'll just get rid of this for you."

She was halfway across the ward when Herbert decided to put his head out for a quick look around. The Ward Sister shrieked and dropped the bottle.

"What on earth is going on?" The Consultant, who had heard the noise while passing, stood at the door. With a shaky hand, the Ward Sister pointed to Herbert who was coolly looking up at them.

"Stand back, everyone," shouted the Consultant, grabbing a long brush that was leaning against the wall. "Look away if you don't like the sight of squashed rodent."

He raised the brush over his head.

There was a humming noise from the direction of Ms Wiz.

Suddenly, the brush seemed to develop a life of its own. It leapt out of the Consultant's hands and pushed

him towards an empty corner bed. As he fell back, the curtains drew around the bed. There were sounds of scuffling.

Not looking particularly alarmed, Herbert sidled down one side of the room and out of the door.

Ms Wiz held up her hands.

"Keep calm," she said. "The rat has left the room. I'm sure he'll turn up—" for a moment she looked worried "—um, somewhere."

"Did you see that brush, Doctor?" gasped the Ward Sister.

"I'm sure there's a perfectly logical explanation for that," said Ms Wiz, walking towards the door.

There were muffled sounds of protest from the corner bed.

"What about the Consultant?" asked the Ward Sister.

Ms Wiz drew back the curtains. The Consultant was swathed head to foot in bandages. He looked like an Egyptian mummy.

"Let me out!" he gasped.

"Someone's going to pay for this!"

"Wow," said Franklyn, as the Consultant was wheeled out of the ward to have his bandages removed. "Your Ms Wiz is the strangest doctor I've ever seen."

"If it wasn't for you, Herbert wouldn't be wandering around the hospital," said Caroline.

"He'll be all right," said Jack. "After all, he's a magic rat."

Franklyn pulled the bedclothes up to his chin. "I'm not letting that Ms Wiz anywhere near me," he said. "She may be a good witch but I don't trust her as a doctor."

Caroline looked at her watch. "We'd better go, Podge," she said.

"Remember we've got to revise for the maths test."

"Wait a minute," he said. "I want to ask Jack a few more questions."

Jack sighed.

"This pain you had," said Podge. "Which side was it on?"

Podge appeared to be deep in thought. He had just had a rather brilliant idea.

CHAPTER FOUR

Lunch on Sunday

Mr Bailey was a worried man.

It was only his second year as a teacher and he was finding it very difficult. The children didn't seem to respect him somehow. Whatever he asked them to do, they did the opposite. They laughed at him behind his back. And they were always playing tricks on him.

That was what happened with Jack Beddows. He had been certain that Jack's stomach ache was just another trick. There was a big maths test on Monday and Jack hated maths.

But it wasn't. The stomach ache was real. Jack was in hospital and Mr Bailey was in trouble.

Mr Gilbert, the head teacher at St

Barnabas, had not been pleased when he heard what had happened.

"I take a dim view, Mr Bailey," he had said. "After all, children are people, you know."

"Are they?" Mr Bailey had said. He wasn't sure any more.

"Why not," the head teacher had sounded tired, "try to be nice for a change?"

"Yes, Mr Gilbert."

Which was why, this Sunday

morning, Mr Bailey was going to visit the hospital. He had bought some flowers and a bunch of grapes and a Get Well card.

Maybe if he was nice to Jack, Class Three would be nice to him. It was worth a try.

Ms Wiz was worried too.

Ever since the Consultant had been pushed around by a brush and wrapped up like a Christmas present, he had been giving her very suspicious looks.

"It's strange," he said, as they did their morning rounds of the wards. "You turn up at the hospital as if by magic, and since then nothing's been quite normal. Bending needles, musical stethoscopes, flying brushes, rats. Where is that animal by the way?"

Ms Wiz shook her head. She hadn't the faintest idea where Herbert was. Secretly, she was afraid that he might decide to investigate the experimental laboratory. He could be quite a mischievous little rat sometimes.

"Yes, it is rather strange," she said.

"What's more, you're never around when real medical work is needed."

Ms Wiz laughed. "Perhaps that's a good thing," she said.

"Morning, nurse," said Jack's father to the Ward Sister as he arrived for his morning visit. "Has he been yet?"

"Dad!" protested Jack.

"Not yet," smiled the Ward Sister. "It takes a while after an appendix operation. Once he moves his bowels, we'll know he's really on the mend."

Bowels?

"What are bowels?" asked Jack's
little sister Jenny.

"Things inside you that move from
time to time," said Mrs Beddows.

"Not very often in Jack's case,"
boomed his father.

Jack noticed a familiar figure
standing at the ward door, looking
confused. At last, Mr Bailey spotted
him.

"Hullo, young lad," he said. "I've
brought you some goodies."

"Thank you," said Jack. "These are my parents and my sister. This is Mr Bailey."

The smile left the teacher's face.

"It . . . it wasn't my fault," he stammered. "They're always saying they've got stomach aches. Or ear aches. Or they feel sick. Particularly when there's a maths test coming up. You don't know who to believe, do you? They're such liars, children. I mean, not Jack – but the others . . . I didn't know it was an appendix. I'm not a doctor, am I? You can't blame me for that . . . can you?"

"Don't worry, Mr Bailey," said Jack's mother. "We all make mistakes."

There was an embarrassed silence.

"So," Jack said eventually. "Who'd like to see my appendix?"

*

It was a tiring morning for Jack. Mr Bailey always had that effect on him and watching him trying to impress his parents somehow made it even worse. So, when a nurse brought him lunch on a tray, he didn't feel the slightest bit hungry.

"Come on, Jack," said his mother. "You'll never get well if you don't eat."

"I just don't feel up to plastic chicken and stringy red cabbage," said Jack.

"Yum," said Mr Bailey loudly. "It looks delicious to me."

Quite why Ms Wiz walked into the ward at this particular moment, Jack never discovered. She was pretending to look at Tom, the boy with grommets, but Jack could tell that she was up to something from the quiet humming noise that was coming from her direction.

The bottle containing his appendix was on a table behind where Mr Bailey and his parents were sitting. This meant that only Jack and Franklyn saw the bottle open quietly. As if it were a real, live caterpillar, the appendix wriggled out.

"Just eat a bit," Jack's father was saying. "A mouthful for each of us."

The appendix crawled along the edge of the table.

"It's getting cold," said his sister.

Jack was speechless. The appendix was making its way on to the lunch tray – and into the red cabbage.

"I know what we'll do," said Mr Bailey. "I'll eat a mouthful, then you eat a mouthful."

"I don't think—"

"Here's a spare spoon," interrupted Franklyn, with an innocent little smile.

"Er, Mr Bailey—" said Jack.

But it was too late. The teacher dipped his spoon into the red cabbage. Jack closed his eyes. When he opened them, Mr Bailey was chewing with a slightly pained smile. The appendix had gone.

"Delicious," said Mr Bailey, swallowing with some difficulty.

Jack glanced over to where Ms Wiz was standing. He really thought she had gone too far this time. She shrugged helplessly.

"That's odd," said Franklyn, pointing at the empty appendix bottle. "Your spare part's gone missing."

"So it has," said Jack.

"Funny how similar to red cabbage it looks," said Franklyn.

Mr Bailey looked at the empty bottle and then at the half-eaten plate of cabbage. Suddenly he felt a little queasy.

"Better be going now," he said, getting unsteadily to his feet.

"Bye, sir," said Jack. "Thanks for coming."

Mr Bailey walked quickly out of the hospital towards his car. It couldn't have been, could it? That red cabbage had tasted a little rubbery.

Perhaps the story would get out. Jack would be bound to spread it around. It would probably get into the local paper. He could see the headlines now. "CRUEL TEACHER EATS BOY'S APPENDIX."

"Why me?" he shouted to an empty car park. He kicked his car, hurting his foot. "Why is it always me?"

CHAPTER FIVE

Mayhem on Monday

Ms Wiz had looked everywhere for Herbert. She had visited all the wards in the hospital. She had checked in the reception hall. She had even searched the kitchen. The only place where she had yet to look was the experimental laboratory, which had been locked up over the weekend.

Now it was Monday morning and Ms Wiz was on her way to the laboratory. It was her last chance. After all, life wouldn't be the same without Herbert.

"Dr Wisdom!"

Ms Wiz heard a familiar voice behind her as she hurried down a corridor. She turned to see the Consultant.

"Where are you going?" he asked.

"I was just looking in on the laboratory," said Ms Wiz. "Er, I'm rather interested in an experiment they're doing."

"You're looking for that rat, aren't you?"

"Rat?"

"You know what I think?" The Consultant put his face close to hers. "I don't think you're a doctor at all. I've seen the way you go pale at the sight of blood. You're never around when I need help with an operation. I think you're an intruder."

Ms Wiz smiled. She was wondering whether she should turn him into a rabbit. Perhaps not, she decided. A rabbit hopping about the hospital with a stethoscope around its neck would make people even more suspicious.

"I'm going to check your papers," said the Consultant. "If it turns out you're not a real doctor, I'm calling the police. Impersonating a doctor – that's serious." He smiled coldly. "They'll probably send you to prison."

Jack was sitting on the edge of his bed. Although his stomach was still sore and he was a bit weak, he was feeling much better. His parents were going to take him home that morning.

115

"So it's goodbye again," said Ms Wiz, who was doing her normal round of the children's ward. "Your stitches will come out in a few days' time and you'll be as good as new."

"Thank you for looking after me," said Jack. "Having an appendix out isn't so bad after all."

"I think you should go and see Mr Bailey as soon as you can," said Ms Wiz. "After all, he visited you."

"Do us some more tricks, Doc," said Franklyn. "I'm going out tomorrow and I'll have something to tell them."

"No more tricks, I'm afraid, Franklyn. I'm leaving today."

"What about Herbert?" asked Jack.

"He'll just have to look after himself," said Ms Wiz. "I can't find him anywhere."

Just then, the doors of the ward opened and the Consultant strode in, his white coat flapping. There were two policemen with him.

"That's her!" he said, pointing at Ms Wiz. "She's the imposter."

"But that's Dr Wisdom," said the Ward Sister.

"Doctor? Hah!" The Consultant's voice echoed round the children's ward as the two policemen advanced towards Ms Wiz.

One of them, who had now produced a notebook, asked, "Are you Doctor, or Miss Dolores Wis—?" At that moment, the swing doors behind the Consultant crashed open and a white tidal wave of live, squeaking creatures poured into the ward.

"What on earth—?" gasped the Consultant.

Mice! Hundreds of them, swarming around the floor, climbing the curtains, exploring every corner. And, in the thick of them, standing up on his hind legs and looking about him, like a general surveying the field of battle, was Herbert.

"There you are, Herbert," said Ms Wiz, reaching down for him. "So you were in the laboratory, after all, were you? Freeing all the mice."

Jack picked his way through the swarm of white mice and whispered something in the Consultant's ear.

"Dr Wisdom," the Consultant shouted over the din. "Rid the hospital of these creatures and you can go free – I'll drop all charges against you."

Ms Wiz raised her hand and whistled. The mice froze, staring at her with little pink eyes. She picked up Herbert and looked around the ward for the last time.

"Thanks, Jack," she said cheerfully. "See you again soon."

"And me, Ms Wiz," said Franklyn.

"Of course. Whenever a bit of magic's needed. Bye everyone." She waved to the other children before making her way out of the ward, followed by Herbert's mouse army.

"And so Ms Wiz saved the hospital from a plague of white mice," Jack told Class Three that afternoon when he visited them. Even Mr Bailey, who had allowed Jack to speak about hospital during a lesson, was looking impressed.

"What will she do with the mice?" asked Caroline.

"Probably lead them to the countryside and set them free," said Jack.

Alex put his hand up. "Can we see your appendix?" he asked. "Caroline said you'd kept it in a bottle."

"Right, back to work, class," Mr Bailey interrupted nervously.

"Oh, I threw it away," said Jack. "Who wants an old piece of gristle anyway?"

He glanced at Mr Bailey, who smiled with relief. Perhaps the head teacher had been right. Children were humans, after all.

"By the way," asked Jack. "Where's Podge?"

An ambulance raced through the streets of the town, its siren blaring and its blue light flashing.

In the back lay the patient, moaning quietly and clutching his right side.

"It worked!" thought Podge, as the ambulance screeched around a corner. He had remembered everything Jack had told him about the appendix, Mr

Bailey had called the doctor, and here
he was on the way to hospital. All he
would have now was a small
operation, five days in hospital with
Ms Wiz looking after him, a few
stitches and that would be that. It
was a small price to pay for missing
the maths test.

The ambulance stopped. The doors
were opened and Podge was wheeled
on a stretcher towards the hospital.

"Hullo, Podge." It was Ms Wiz, with

Hecate under her arm. "What's up?"

"Appendix, Ms Wiz," groaned Podge.

Hecate's eyes lit up.

"Oh dear. What a pity I'm just going," said Ms Wiz. "In fact, I only came back to collect Hecate."

"Going?"

"So you'll just have to face your major operation all on your own."

Podge gulped. "Er, maybe . . ."

Ms Wiz laughed. "Lend us your stretcher, Podge," she said.

Podge thought for a moment, and then rolled off the stretcher.

"Oh well," he said. "It was worth a try."

"Thanks, Podge," said Ms Wiz, climbing on. The stretcher rose and hovered over the heads of the ambulance men.

"I'll be back – when you're least expecting me," she called out as the

stretcher rose higher, turned slowly and floated over the roof of the hospital and out of sight.

As Podge and the ambulance men watched Ms Wiz disappear, a nurse walked out of the hospital. She had a clipboard under her arm.

"Well, young man," she said. "Let's get you registered. How's the pain now?"

"Better, thank you," said Podge. "Suddenly much better."

You're Nicked, Ms Wiz

CHAPTER ONE

A Sort of Missing Person

"Daydreaming *again*, Lizzie Thompson?"

The words came to Lizzie from far away. She had been staring out of the window into the playground at St Barnabas School, unaware that her class teacher Mr Bailey was standing in front of her desk.

"Sorry, sir," she said quietly. "I was thinking about my cat."

"Your what?"

"My cat. Waif."

"Oh I see," said Mr Bailey. "Here we all are in the middle of an English lesson, discussing similes, and Lizzie's off in a private fantasy about her cat. That's absolutely fine then, isn't it?"

"It's lost, sir," said Jack, who was one of Lizzie's best friends. "It disappeared yesterday."

"Well, staring out of the window's not going to help, is it?" said the teacher briskly.

"Cruel," muttered Podge at the back of the class. "How would he like it?"

Mr Bailey thumped Lizzie's desk. "I would like it if Class Three did some *work* for a change," he said loudly. "Now, back to similes. Here is an example of a simile: 'Podge sits at his desk like a sack of potatoes.' Now who can give me another simile?"

Caroline put up her hand.

"Our teacher is like someone who doesn't know how you feel when you lose a pet and then he can't even manage to be nice when a person's so upset that she can't concentrate on a boring English lesson, especially when it's taught by a cat-hater. Or is that a metaphor, sir?"

Everybody in Class Three laughed – except for Lizzie, who was looking out of the window again.

After school, Lizzie ran home, hoping for the best but fearing the worst. All day, she had been unable to think of anything but Waif. Now, as she ran, she remembered the winter's day when she had found him, cold, shivering and hungry, among the dustbins by her house. He had hardly been more than a kitten. When no one came to feed him after a few days, she took him in. "Waif" she had called him.

And now he was gone.

"I've looked everywhere," said Lizzie's mother, when she arrived home. "In cupboards. Down the street. In the park—" she hesitated. "Under cars."

Tears welled up in Lizzie's eyes.

"You think he's dead, don't you?" she said.

Mrs Thompson put her arm around her daughter. "It's dangerous for cats around here. People drive so fast," she said, adding gently, "He's had a good innings."

"He's only six, Mummy," sobbed Lizzie. "Since when has six been a good innings?"

She ran upstairs to her room and slammed the door.

The next morning, Lizzie did something she had never done before. After waving goodbye to her mother at the end of her street, she walked towards St Barnabas as usual but, instead of turning right towards the High Street where she normally met Jack and Caroline, she turned left into the park.

"I just know that Waif is alive," she muttered to herself, "and today I'm going to find him."

"Good for you, dear," said an old tramp woman who was sitting on a park bench nearby, but Lizzie was too deep in thought to pay her any attention.

Lizzie's plan to find Waif went like this:

1. Look under a lot of bushes.
2. Pin up on trees the notices she had written late last night. They read: "LOST: BEAUTIFUL WHITE CAT WITH GINGER PATCHES (MALE). ANSWERS TO NAME OF WAIF (OR WAIFY). MUCH LOVED. IF FOUND, PLEASE PHONE 579 8282."

3. Go to the police station and ask
   for their help.

But nothing went right. All morning,
Lizzie looked under bushes without
success. She pinned up her notices,
but then there were so many other
lost cat notices that she began to
despair.

"Everyone round here seems to
have lost a cat recently," she sighed.

Finally, late that afternoon, she
stumbled into the local police station.

"And what can I do for you, young
lady?" asked the police constable
behind the desk.

"I've lost my cat," said Lizzie
nervously.

The policeman chuckled, as if he'd
just been told a rather good joke.

"D'you know what this is, young
lady?" he said, tapping a big book in
front of him. "It's called the Crime

Book. In this book, I note down all the really terrible things that people get up to in this area. Theft, hit and run, breaking and entering, bag-snatching, vagrancy, motor offences, missing persons, grievous bodily harm – all sorts of nastiness."

"I see," said Lizzie.

"And now you want me to add to the list of ongoing, unsolved misdemeanours one little moggie that's gone walkabout, right?"

"He's a sort of missing person, too."

"Listen, miss. I know cats. They wander. Especially toms."

"He's not a tom," said Lizzie. "He's . . . neuter."

The policeman looked confused. "New to what?" he asked. "If he's new to the area, no wonder he's lost."

"PC Boote." Another policeman,

who had overheard the conversation, now joined them. He winked at Lizzie. "When the young lady says her cat's neuter, I think she means that he's—" He whispered into the police constable's ear.

"Oh dear, oh dear," said PC Boote, wincing slightly. He turned to Lizzie. "When did this, er, neutering happen then?"

"Don't worry, miss," said the

second policeman quickly. "We'll let you know if we hear of a lost cat. Just give PC Boote here the details."

Sighing heavily, PC Boote noted in the Crime Book Lizzie's name, telephone number and her description of Waif.

"Looking for lost cats," he muttered. "I've heard it all now."

Lizzie turned to leave. Somehow finding Waif was turning out to be even more difficult than she thought it was going to be.

Miserably, she stood on the steps of the police station, wondering what to do next.

"What you need is a spot of magic," said a familiar voice. It was the tramp who had seen Lizzie in the park. She was pushing a pram full of old rags, on which sat a china cat with odd, glowing eyes.

"Thanks," sniffed Lizzie. "And

where exactly do you find magic these days?"

"Follow me," said the tramp.

CHAPTER TWO

A Strange Coincidence

Mr Bailey was panicking.

Yesterday, Lizzie Thompson had been upset about her cat. And what had he done? He had shouted, told her to get on with her work and hit the desk with his hand. And now Lizzie was absent from class. He had gone too far yet again. He would just have to ask the head teacher to ring her mother.

Mrs Thompson was panicking. When the head teacher had rung to find out whether Lizzie was ill, she had been at work. It was three in the afternoon before she found out that her daughter had been missing all day. Then she rang the police.

PC Boote was panicking.

As soon as the report of a missing girl came through, he realised that this was the very same girl he had seen that afternoon.

"And what happened to her, police constable?" asked the station sergeant.

"She walked out of the station, sarge," mumbled PC Boote.

"And?"

"Er, I think I might have seen her walking off with a tramp."

The police sergeant sighed and reached for a telephone. This could be serious – very serious indeed.

"But I don't understand why you're all dressed in rags, Ms Wiz."

Lizzie and the tramp woman were sitting in a dingy café, drinking tea. Outside, it was already getting dark. An old man at the next table was darting suspicious looks in their direction as he shook a tomato ketchup bottle over his egg and chips.

"The last time I saw you," Lizzie continued, "you were a teacher."

Ms Wiz smiled.

"Do you remember what I told you then?" she asked. "I said I'd be back whenever a spot of magic was needed. So here I am."

"I see," said Lizzie quietly. She was beginning to wonder whether she was right to be here, sitting in a café with Ms Wiz. A worrying thought had occurred to her. Maybe it was somebody *pretending* to be Ms Wiz. What if this was the Danger Stranger she had always been told never to talk to?

"Watch," said the tramp woman, as if she could read Lizzie's mind.

There was a low hum from where she was sitting.

"Blimey!" said the man sitting at

the next-door table as the contents
of the tomato ketchup bottle covered
his plate.

"That's not magic," said Lizzie.
"That's life."

There was a slurping noise as the
ketchup disappeared back into the
bottle.

"*Blimey*!" gasped the man.

"Ms Wiz!" said Lizzie, laughing for
the first time that day. "You never
change, do you?"

"Only in the way I look," said Ms Wiz, taking a notebook from her pocket. "Now let's get down to business."

"D'you want a pen?" asked Lizzie.

"That won't be necessary," said Ms Wiz. "Cat's name?"

"Waif."

"Missing for how long?"

"Two days."

"Distinguishing features?"

"Green eyes, lovely white coat with

ginger patches . . ." Lizzie sighed as she remembered Waif. "Very friendly."

"Other facts known?"

"Only that everyone round here seems to have lost a cat."

"Mmm." Ms Wiz looked thoughtful. "Seems a strange coincidence."

"Yes," said Lizzie. "It is strange and all the lost cat notices mentioned that they had nice coats. That seemed a bit odd."

"Odd," said Ms Wiz, "and worrying. It's time for us to get moving."

"Aren't you going to note anything down?" asked Lizzie.

"Whoops, silly me," said Ms Wiz, staring hard at the notebook. As if an invisible hand were writing, the page quickly filled up with notes. "There you go," she said briskly.

Lizzie shook her head. Nothing was

ever straightforward when Ms Wiz was around. "Now what do we do?" she asked.

"I'm going to tell you our plan," said Ms Wiz. "But before that, we're going to write to your mother, who'll be worrying about you. Then we're going home."

"To *your* home?" Lizzie couldn't believe her ears. When she was a teacher, Ms Wiz had always been very mysterious about where she lived and no one from Class Three had been invited back.

"It's not much," shrugged Ms Wiz, "but I think you'll like it."

It was dark by the time a letter from Lizzie was slipped under Mrs Thompson's door.

It read:

Dear Mum

Please don't worry about me. I'm alright and I've met up with someone who's going to use magic to help me find Waif.

Do you remember Ms Wiz, our magical teacher? People called her a witch but she always said that she was a Paranormal operative. Well, it's her. Except now she's a tramp.

I'm staying at Ms Wiz's home, so everything is alright.

Love

Lizzie
xxx

PS Don't get the police to look for us. They probably wouldn't recognize me since Ms Wiz's plan is to turn me into a cat!!!

Mrs Thompson read the note again.
Slowly the awful truth began to sink
in.

Her only daughter had run off with
a tramp . . .

Or maybe a witch . . .

And she was about to be turned
into a cat . . . !

With a little cry, Mrs Thompson ran
to telephone the police.

CHAPTER THREE

Magic – or Trouble?

"Is this it?"

Lizzie was unable to keep the disappointment from her voice when they reached Ms Wiz's home.

Because it wasn't really a home at all. It was an extremely old car with flat tyres and dents all over it. It did have curtains but even they were more like rags, hung over the windows to stop people peering in.

"Yes, this is it," said Ms Wiz proudly. "What d'you think?"

"Interesting," said Lizzie, who didn't want to hurt Ms Wiz's feelings. "Not quite what I expected but . . . interesting."

"If you like it now, just wait until you step inside."

Ms Wiz opened the door with a flourish. Lizzie gasped.

From the outside, Ms Wiz's car had looked no more than a tangle of rusty, useless metal, just the sort of place where you might expect a tramp to live, but inside . . .

. . . it was even worse. All that Lizzie could see were torn, grey rugs, old newspapers and half-eaten sandwiches. Then something moved on the back seat – something small and grey.

"A rat!" Lizzie screamed.

"Of course," said Ms Wiz. "Don't you remember Herbert, my magic rat?"

She picked up Herbert and clambered into the car. "You can use the guest bedroom," she said, pointing to the back seat. Reluctantly, Lizzie climbed in.

"Close the door behind you," said Ms Wiz.

Something very strange happened as Lizzie pulled the door shut. There was a low hum and, as if someone had thrown a switch somewhere, the car started changing. The front seats turned around and became small armchairs. A table with crisps and lemonade appeared out of the floor. The back seat became a sofa. And the gearstick was transformed into a lamp which lit up the inside of the car with a soft pink glow.

Lizzie couldn't believe her eyes. It was as if she was no longer in a rusty old wreck of a car but in a warm country cottage.

"Being a paranormal operative has its advantages," smiled Ms Wiz.

"What are we going to do now?" asked Lizzie, settling down on the sofa. She was beginning to feel sleepy.

"We'll wait up for the catnappers," said Ms Wiz.

"Catnappers?"

"That's where your Waif has gone," said Ms Wiz. "And those other cats. They've been kidnapped, I'm sure of it."

"But why?"

"Gloves," said Ms Wiz grimly. "Fur gloves. That's why all the cats that have disappeared have nice coats."

Suddenly Lizzie felt afraid. Looking under bushes was one thing. But staying up all night to catch a

gang of catnappers? For a moment, she wished she was back in her bed, safe.

"Help yourself to crisps," said Ms Wiz, peering through the curtains into the darkness of the park outside. "I'll keep look-out. All the local cats come to this park at night and I have a feeling that our friends the catnappers will be here too. They'll lead us to Waif."

"How do you know he's alive?" Lizzie asked.

"Let's just put it down to intuition," said Ms Wiz.

Lizzie felt braver now. After all, she was with Ms Wiz. They had magic on their side.

"Jack, a policeman's here to ask you some questions."

Jack Beddows had just been dozing off when his mother switched on the light. There, in his bedroom, stood a policeman with a notebook in his hand.

"Sorry to interrupt your beauty sleep, young man," said PC Boote, "but we have a small emergency concerning your friend Lizzie."

Jack rubbed his eyes. "What's happened to her?" he asked.

"Her mother has received a letter

which gives us reason to believe
that she has been abducted by a
certain—" PC Boote looked in his
notebook "—Ms Wiz."

"Ms Wiz!" Jack sat up in his bed.
"Where is she?"

"That's the problem," said PC
Boote. "At first we thought she was
just a tramp but now it turns out that
she's an all-round troublemaker. We
think Lizzie's gone off with her."

"That's all right then," said Jack.

"All right?" PC Boote seemed surprised. "According to information received, this Ms Wiz has in the past turned teachers into geese, removed a school inspector's trousers and released about a thousand white mice into the children's ward of a general hospital. That's not what I call all right."

"Ms Wiz is magic," said Jack.

PC Boote put on his most serious expression. "You call it magic, son," he said. "I call it trouble. Now, we need to know exactly what she looks like.

"Here we go," said Ms Wiz, peering through the curtains of her car.

A van drew up by the gates of the park. Two men in dark clothes stepped out and climbed over the

158

railings. The younger and taller of the two men was carrying a net while the other, a short, elderly man with a slight limp, followed him, whistling softly.

"Come on then," whispered Ms Wiz, shaking Lizzie by the shoulder.

"Mmmm?" said Lizzie sleepily.

"Our friends are here," said Ms Wiz. "It's time to put our plan into action."

After no more than half an hour, the men returned. They were carrying two cats, trapped in the net.

"This tabby puss is a young 'un," said the older man. "Shall I let it go?"

"Young or old, makes no difference," said the other man, opening the back of the van and bundling the cats into a sack. "And stop calling them 'puss'. Sometimes I think you're too soft for this game."

"What do we do now?" Lizzie

whispered as, moments later, the van began to move.

"Follow them, of course," answered Ms Wiz. "Just because my home's got four flat tyres, it doesn't mean it can't go."

And, sure enough, the old car seemed to raise itself slightly at that moment and, as if hovering just above the ground, moved quietly forward to follow the van.

"The moment we arrive, we put our plan into action," said Ms Wiz as they drove quietly down the dark streets, always keeping a safe distance from the catnappers in front of them.

"Right," said Lizzie quietly. She was thinking of her mother, and how worried she would be. Still, there was no going back now.

Ms Wiz glanced over her shoulder.

"Nervous?" she asked.

"Not really," Lizzie lied. "So long as you're there to help."

Soon the van drew up outside a large dark house with closed shutters.

"I know this place," whispered Lizzie. "It's called the Old Hospital."

"All right," said Ms Wiz, stopping the car. "Ready?"

The men were getting out and opening the back of the van.

"Ready," said Lizzie, closing her eyes.

There was a low hum from the front of the car. Lizzie felt as if she had been slapped hard on the back. When she opened her eyes, everything in the car was bigger. She was looking up at Ms Wiz, who was smiling.

"What a lovely cat," Ms Wiz said. "Now remember the plan. You follow them into the house and, as soon as you're alone with the cats, scratch your left ear three times. I'll be outside and, as soon as I get that message, I'll turn you back into Lizzie again. Then you let the cats out, all right?"

"Sure," said Lizzie with a cat smile. To her surprise, she found that she could still talk in her normal voice.

The men were carrying the sack up the steps to the house when Lizzie, now a sleek black cat, went after them.

As they opened the door, she slipped in behind them.

Ms Wiz stood by her car, staring up at the house. "Good luck, Lizzie," she muttered.

It was then that she felt a heavy hand on her shoulder.

"You're nicked, Ms Wiz," said PC Boote.

CHAPTER FOUR

Abandoned

It wasn't bad being a cat, Lizzie discovered.

Nobody noticed you, for example. You could creep under tables and hide in the shadows. You could jump onto window-ledges, as if it were the most natural thing in the world. And, even if you did lose your balance, you always seemed to land on your feet. It was quite fun.

Or at least it would have been if Lizzie had been in a normal house rather than in a catnappers' den.

Lizzie quickly discovered where they kept the cats. The older of the catnappers had trudged down to the cellar with the sack on his back. There was an unearthly yowling sound as a door was opened.

"There you go, my lovelies," he said. "Good puss." Lizzie heard hissing and scrabbling as the two new cats were bundled into the room. She ducked under a chair as the man returned, carrying an empty sack.

"That's about it then," he said to the other catnapper. "Mrs D'Arcy from the fur shop will be along tomorrow morning to tell us which ones she needs. Then," – for a moment he looked almost sad – "it's bye-bye, pussies."

"This is the last time I take you on a job," said the younger man. "Honestly, a catnapper that likes cats! I've heard it all now."

The older man sniffed. "I feel sorry for them, that's all. You wouldn't understand."

"If you like them so much, you'd better feed them."

The man fetched a paper sack of cat food and calling out, "Din-dins, pussies," he limped down the stairs. Lizzie followed.

For a moment, as he opened the door and threw some food in, there was total confusion in the room – and, in that moment, Lizzie slipped in.

What she saw took her breath away.

There were cats everywhere. Some were fighting over the food, some were miaowing pitifully, some were pacing backwards and forwards, some were simply asleep. One or two of the cats, startled to hear a human voice coming from a cat, arched their backs and hissed nervously.

"Don't worry," said Lizzie, carefully stepping through the throng of cats. "I'm just looking for someone. I'm not really a cat myself."

167

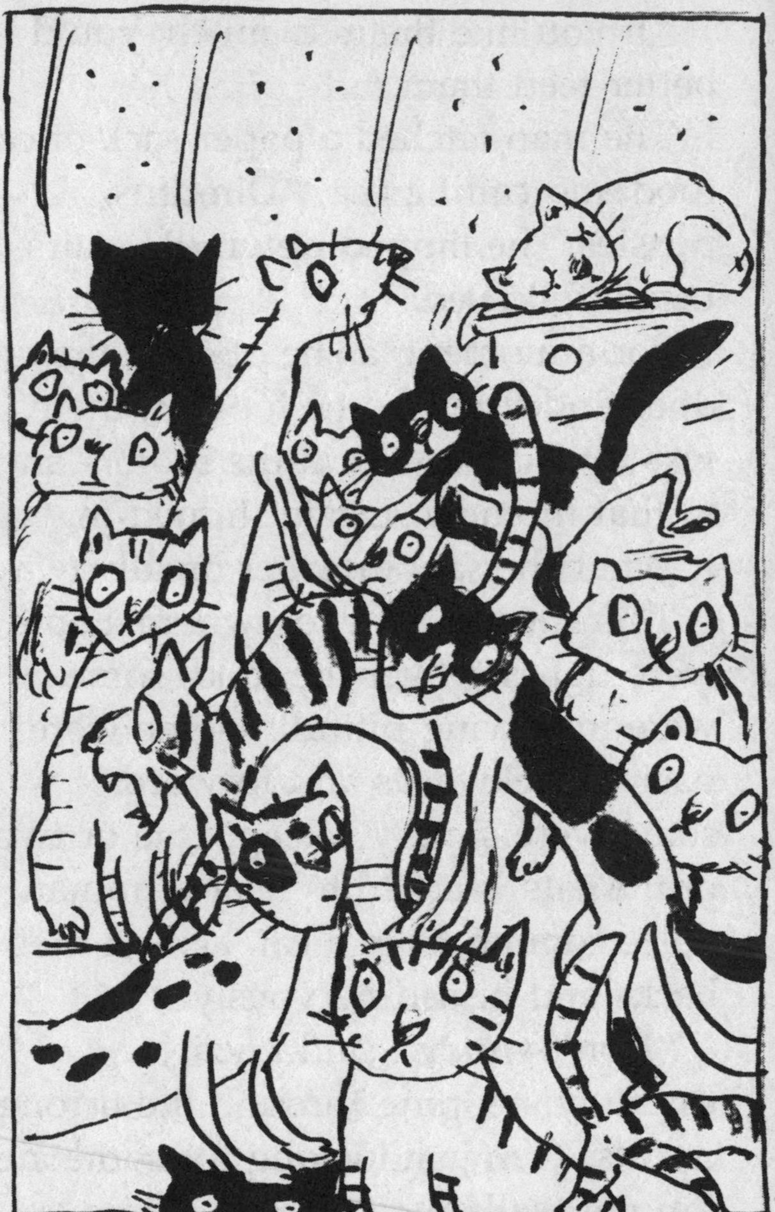

At that moment, a big ginger tom stepped forward and cuffed her around the ear.

"Ow!" said Lizzie. Without thinking she tapped him back, leaving her claws out. Surprised, the tom retreated backwards into a tabby, which bit him.

"Stop fighting, you stupid animals," said Lizzie angrily. "Don't you realise that tomorrow you could be . . ." At that moment, Lizzie saw a familiar white form in a corner. "Waif?"

The white cat stirred, recognising the voice, and gave a soft miaow. Lizzie looked closer. Yes it was Waif – asleep as usual.

It was time for action. Soon the catnappers would be going to bed. All Lizzie needed to do was to give Ms Wiz the signal to turn her back into a human, sneak out of the door, and then lead the cats to freedom.

Bracing herself for the shock, Lizzie scratched herself three times behind the left ear.

Nothing happened.

"Come on, Ms Wiz," she muttered, trying to keep calm. "Get that magic working." She scratched again, harder this time.

But nothing happened.

"Ms Wiz, where are you?" With growing desperation, Lizzie scratched and scratched and scratched.

But absolutely nothing happened.

"Don't you understand? Magic doesn't work at long distance. I can't change Lizzie back into a little girl from here."

Ms Wiz was sitting in a small, white-walled room at the police station. For the past hour, she had been trying to explain to PC Boote exactly why she needed to return to the catnappers' house as soon as possible.

"I see," said the police constable. "So your, er, magic is a bit like my walkie-talkie, is it? You have to be in range for it to work."

Ms Wiz sighed wearily. Why was it that grown-ups found it so difficult to understand magic when children found it so easy?

"That's right," she said.

"And you expect me to believe that you've cast a spell—" PC Boote could hardly keep the disbelief out of his voice "—transforming Lizzie Thompson into a cat in order to save a load of moggies from a couple of nasty men who want to turn them into gloves. And that's why you were at the Old Hospital."

"Precisely," said Ms Wiz.

"You must think I'm daft."

Ms Wiz was about to reply when the door opened. It was the station sergeant.

"Any luck, constable?" he asked.

"I'm afraid not," said PC Boote. "We're still in the land of witches and wizards."

"Right," said the sergeant. "She can spend the night in the cells. Tomorrow morning we've got two of Lizzie's classmates coming in to tell us whether this really is the famous Ms Wiz."

"You don't seem to understand," said Ms Wiz. "Tomorrow could be too late."

PC Boote turned to the sergeant and, with a grim little smile, tapped the side of his head.

At first, when they were led into the small room at the police station, Jack

and Caroline didn't recognise Ms Wiz.
After a worried, sleepless night in the
cells, she looked more like a tired,
dishevelled tramp than ever.

Then she smiled.

"Ms Wiz!" said Caroline, hugging
her.

"You look so different," said Jack.

"Hullo, Caroline and Jack," said Ms
Wiz. "Could you explain to this
policeman who I am?"

But, as the children told PC Boote about Ms Wiz, he continued to look suspicious.

"I'll need to discuss this with my superiors," he said eventually.

"There's no time for that," said Ms Wiz angrily. She turned to the children. "Do either of you know the way to the Old Hospital?"

"I do," said Jack.

Suddenly the sound of a low hum

filled the room. PC Boote was just about to speak when something very odd happened. He turned into a white rabbit.

"Sorry about that," said Ms Wiz, unlocking the door to the room with the keys that were now on the floor. "Let's go, children."

The police station now appeared to be completely empty, except for a number of white rabbits.

"Did you have to turn the whole police force into rabbits?" asked Jack as they hurried out of the main entrance. "There's going to be terrible trouble."

"I couldn't mess around," said Ms Wiz briskly. "This is a matter of life and death."

"Why didn't you do it earlier then?" asked Caroline.

"I didn't know the way to the Old Hospital," said Ms Wiz. "I may be magic but my sense of direction is terrible."

Outside the station stood a police car. Ms Wiz opened the car door and, pushing a white rabbit aside, leapt into the driver's seat.

"Jump in!" she shouted. The police car's engine started with a roar. "Let's just hope we're in time."

CHAPTER FIVE

Fur Free

A thin ray of light penetrated the gloom of the cellar at the Old Hospital. Lizzie lay dozing, curled up beside Waif. Her left ear was sore from where she had been scratching all night. She was frightened.

Some of the cats around her stirred restlessly as they heard the sound of footsteps approaching the cellar. The door was flung open to reveal the most extraordinary woman Lizzie had ever seen. She was very tall and was wearing fur from head to foot.

"Ugh, disgusting!" said the woman. "If there's one thing I hate, it's live creatures."

"Think of them as pelts, Mrs D'Arcy," said the younger catnapper

nervously. "That's what they will be soon."

Mrs D'Arcy looked around the room.

"Frankly," she said, "there are some pelts here that I wouldn't allow my chauffeur to clean my car with."

The older man looked shocked. "Madam uses fur on her car?" he asked.

"I use fur for everything," said Mrs D'Arcy with a dangerous smile.

"Every item of clothing that I wear was once alive." She stroked her soft mink coat. "Now – let's get down to business. Count these horrible animals and I'll tell you how much I can pay."

The police car arrived at the Old Hospital with a squeal of brakes.

"Look, Ms Wiz!" said Jack, pointing to a large grey Rolls Royce, with a number plate which read "FUR 1", which was parked outside the front door.

"Just as I feared," said Ms Wiz, jumping out. "The fur merchant is here. Come on!"

Jack and Caroline followed her up the steps. Without hesitating, Ms Wiz kicked the front door, causing it to open with a loud crack.

"Wow," said Caroline. "Magic!"

"No," said Ms Wiz grimly. "That wasn't magic. That was anger."

Just then the older catnapper limped up the stairs from the cellar.

" 'Ere, what are you lot doing?" he said.

"We're here for the cats, so don't try and stop us," said Ms Wiz.

The old man smiled. "Stop you rescuing my little pussies? Why would I do that?" He winked as he walked past them towards the door. "I'll leave you to it. Good luck."

"Was *that* magic?" asked Jack.

"No, I think it was something called conscience," replied Ms Wiz.

At that moment, the three of them became aware of someone else climbing the stairs towards them.

"I don't know who you are," said a loud voice from the darkness in front of them. "But my name is Mrs D'Arcy. I'm very rich, very powerful and, when I'm annoyed, I can be very unpleasant."

"Careful, Ms Wiz," whispered Jack. "She looks as if she means it."

"We want those cats," Ms Wiz called out. "Open that door right now."

Mrs D'Arcy laughed. "I'm sure you do," she said. "From the way you're dressed, you look as if you could use a fur coat."

"I'm fur free," said Ms Wiz, moving closer.

"That's quite far enough," warned Mrs D'Arcy. "You're probably absolutely filthy. I don't want any nasty marks on my fur coat."

"What fur coat?" asked Ms Wiz innocently, as the sound of a low hum filled the basement stairs.

Automatically, Mrs D'Arcy touched her coat – and gasped. The fur was beginning to move, as if it had a life of its own.

"What's happening?" she said, going pale.

"Nothing much," said Ms Wiz. "I'll release the cats in a moment. But first of all, I want to free the animals that made your coat."

Before Jack's and Caroline's astonished eyes, Mrs D'Arcy's clothes were becoming a writhing mass of animals.

"But everything I'm wearing is fur," she shrieked.

"Oh dear," said Ms Wiz. "How very embarrassing."

By now, Mrs D'Arcy's coat had completely disappeared and several small, furry animals were shaking and scratching themselves at her feet. With a scream, she ran up the stairs, as the rest of her clothes began to turn back into animals.

Ms Wiz opened the door to the cellar. The second of the two catnappers was standing, apparently unable to move, in the middle of the room. One of the cats had gone to sleep on his feet.

"I thought of turning him into a mouse," said Ms Wiz. "But in the end I decided on a human statue. Cats can be so cruel."

"There's Waif!" shouted Caroline, pointing across the room.

"Never mind Waif," said Jack. "What about Lizzie?"

At that moment, a sleek black cat stretched sleepily and scratched herself three times behind the left ear.

"Lizzie!"

Within moments of becoming a human being again, Lizzie had telephoned her mother. Now, minutes later, mother and daughter were hugging each other joyfully on the steps of the Old Hospital.

"Where's Waif?" asked Mrs Thompson.

"He's being fed in the kitchen with the other cats," said Jack. "We're going to hold on to them until we can find all their owners."

"And who on earth is that odd woman hiding in the Rolls Royce without any clothes on?"

Lizzie laughed. "It's a long story," she said. "Perhaps Ms Wiz had better explain it. Where is she, by the way?"

"Oh no!" said Jack, who had noticed Ms Wiz's battered old car rising slowly off its flat tyres like a hovercraft about to move off. "She can't go now."

A white rabbit was hopping busily down the road towards them.

"Ms Wiz!" shouted Lizzie. "You've forgotten the police! They're still rabbits!"

The car hesitated and hovered with a low hum.

"All right," said PC Boote, shaking himself as if he had just awoken from a rather strange dream. "Where are these catnappers then?"

"The ringleader's over there," said Lizzie, pointing to Mrs D'Arcy's car. "But she's—"

"No buts," said the policeman. "Leave this to me."

He walked slowly towards the Rolls Royce.

"Right, you in there," he said, bending down to look in the window. "You're nicked. Er, you're nacked. Oh no, you're absolutely n-n-n-naked!"

He turned away, blushing.

And everyone, even PC Boote, started laughing.